¡Perros! ¡Perros!
Dogs! Dogs!

BY Ginger Foglesong Guy

PICTURES BY Sharon Glick

rayo

Greenwillow Books, An Imprint of HarperCollinsPublishers

¡Perros! ¡Perros! Dogs! Dogs!
Text copyright © 2006 by Ginger Foglesong Guy
Illustrations copyright © 2006 by Sharon Glick
All rights reserved. Manufactured in China.
www.harpercollinschildrens.com
Rayo is an imprint of HarperCollins Publishers, Inc.

Watercolors and black ink were used for the full-color art.
The text type is Goudy Sans Medium.

Library of Congress Cataloging-in-Publication Data
Guy, Ginger Foglesong.
¡Perros! ¡Perros! Dogs! Dogs! / by Ginger Foglesong Guy ;
pictures by Sharon Glick.
    p.   cm.
"Greenwillow Books."
ISBN-10: 0-06-083574-5 (trade bdg.). ISBN-13: 978-0-06-083574-3 (trade bdg.)
ISBN-10: 0-06-083575-3 (lib. bdg.) ISBN-13: 978-0-06-083575-0 (lib. bdg.)
1. Spanish language—Synonyms and antonyms—Juvenile literature. I. Glick, Sharon. II. Title.
PC4591.G89 2006 468.1—dc22 2005040439

First Edition 10 9 8 7 6 5 4 3 2 1

 Greenwillow Books

rayo

For June and Aldo
—G. F. G.

To Jessie
—S. G.

¡Perros! ¡Perros!
Dogs! Dogs!

¡Muchos perros!
Lots of dogs!

Perro grande. Perro chico.
Big dog. Little dog.

¿Adónde van?   Where are they going?

Arriba, abajo.
Up, down.
Por el pueblo.
Through the town.

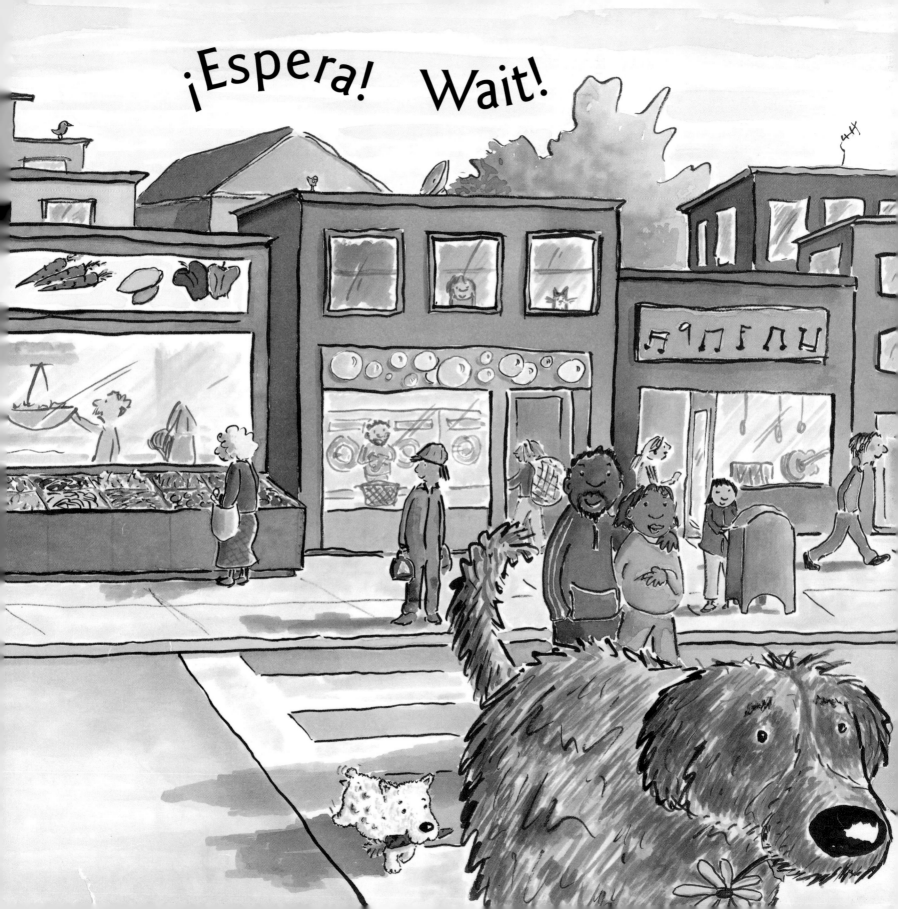

¡Más perros!
More dogs!
Perro ancho. Perro estrecho.
Wide dog. Narrow dog.

¿Adónde van?   Where are they going?

Arriba, abajo.
Up, down.
Por el pueblo.
Through the town.

¡Espera! Wait!

¡Más y más perros!
More and more dogs!
Perro rápido. Perro lento.
Fast dog. Slow dog.

Perro limpio. Perro sucio.
Clean dog. Dirty dog.

¿Adónde van?   Where are they going?

Arriba, abajo.
Up, down.
Por el pueblo.
Through the town.

¡Más y más y más perros!
More and more and more dogs!

Perro mojado. Perro seco.
Wet dog. Dry dog.

Perro negro. Perro blanco.
Black dog. White dog.
Perro liso. Perro rizado.
Smooth dog. Curly dog.

Arriba, abajo.
Up, down.

Por el pueblo.
Through the town.

Ladrando.
Barking.

Brincando.
Jumping.